Vampires
and Other Creatures
of the Night

**Look for other scary stories
you might enjoy:**

13 Ghostly Tales
Freya Littledale

Tales for the Midnight Hour
J.B. Stamper

13 Ghosts: Strange but True Stories
Will Osborne

Vampires
and Other Creatures
of the Night

by Rita Golden Gelman and Nancy Lamb
illustrated by C.B. Mordan

SCHOLASTIC INC.
New York Toronto London Auckland Sydney

For Ben and Noah, Mitch and Jan —
and all the other children in the world
who have encountered
monsters in the night

ISBN 0-590-44302-X

12 11 10 9 8 7 6 5   5 6/9

Printed in the U.S.A.   40

First Scholastic printing, October 1991

Contents

Out of the Night

There have always been scary beasts of the night . . . in the legends, in the minds, and perhaps in the forests and graveyards of human history.

- Eerie monsters that rise out of coffins, looking for blood to quench their thirst.
- Furry creatures that stalk through the dark, hunting flesh for gruesome feasts.
- Wicked beasts that hide under beds, waiting to grab an innocent sleeper.

For as long as there have been humans, there have been monsters to torment them.

Psychologists say that people make up these monsters to explain things they don't understand — things like weird sounds and grisly deaths. It's easier to create a "real" monster, such as a vampire or werewolf, than to think there is an unknown horror lurking in the dark.

Most likely, vampires, werewolves, and other beasts that stalk through the night are creatures of the mind; they don't really exist.

So the psychologists say.

But the people who told the tales in this book would have had trouble believing the psychologists. These people claimed to have heard the werewolves howl, to have seen the bloody corpses of vampires, to have felt the grasping fingers of the beast under the bed.

For these people, the monsters were very real.

Vampires

"What should you do if you suspect you've been bitten by a vampire?"
"Drink some water and see if your neck leaks."

•

Said the vampire mother to her vampire children: "Stop fighting and eat your soup before it clots."

•

"Vampires and teenagers are a lot alike: They're both misunderstood."
— *A bumper sticker*

According to the Legends

Vampires are dead people who don't stay dead. By day they "live" quietly in their coffins; at night they rise from their graves and go in search of their favorite food — human blood.

Vampires get their nourishment by biting people on the neck and sucking out their blood.

There are stories about vampires from all parts of the world. And in most of those stories vampires are evil. They cause sickness and epidemics, strange behavior and sudden death.

Vampires come in different colors. They come in different shapes and sizes, too. And their behavior varies from place to place. But there's one nasty habit that all vampires share: an uncontrollable lust for human blood.

So say the legends.

Getting to Know Vampires

Vampires are female and male, black and white. Farmers, soldiers, noblemen. Mothers, fathers, kids. They're actually pretty ordinary folk . . . or they were, before they became vampires.

Often they have long canine teeth that they use to pierce the skin of their victims. Vampires in Poland have pointed barbs at the tips of their tongues, similar to a bee's stinger.

Some legends tell about vampires who are pale

and deathlike; others say the skin of a vampire is abnormally red, especially after it has just eaten.

Lots of vampires have glaring eyes . . . sometimes deep and dark, sometimes fiery red, and sometimes blue. Whatever the color of their eyes, vampires can see in the dark.

Bulgarian vampires have only one nostril. Greek vampires have skin that's stretched so tightly across the bones it can be played like a drum. And Chinese vampires are thought to have white or greenish fur on their bodies.

Many of the legends say that vampires have clawlike nails and stringy hair, even on the palms of their hands. They have dirty fingernails, too, all caked with dried blood.

There are numerous reports that vampires have disgustingly bad breath and a repulsive body odor. One writer said that a particular vampire had "a most grievous stink . . . beyond all imagination and expression." There's also a story about the English vampire, the Squire of Alwick Castle. Wherever he went, he spread the smell of "death and rotting flesh."

Some people say that vampires are icy cold before they eat, and feverish afterwards. But others claim that vampires are *always* cold to the touch.

Another curious thing about vampires is that when they stand in front of a mirror, there is no reflection; and when they stand in front of a light, they cast no shadow. For mirror images and shadows have always been believed to be reflections of the soul. And vampires have no soul.

Everyone knows that vampires drink blood, and they usually attack while their victims are asleep. What's not commonly known is that vampires can hypnotize their victims. Usually people don't even know they've been bitten. When they wake up in the morning, they think they've had a bad dream . . . until they discover teeth marks on their necks.

Vampire victims become weak and sick. Usually they die . . . but only briefly. For victims of the vampire's bite are almost certain to become vampires themselves.

So say the legends.

The Story of Arnold Paoli

In 1727, the story goes, Arnold Paoli was in the army, stuck in a little village in Greece that everyone said was infested with vampires.

Hordes of villagers had moved away. The ones who couldn't leave protected themselves with garlic and crosses, which were said to keep vampires away.

One night, in spite of his precautions, Arnold was bitten. He didn't even know it had happened until the next morning when he discovered the marks on his neck.

Arnold didn't die immediately. As soon as he realized what had happened, he ran to the cemetery and began digging up graves and opening coffins, for he had heard that he might save himself from "vampirehood" if he dug up and "killed" the vampire who bit him. Over and over again he found bones and decayed bodies and more bones, until finally he found a vampire. He knew it was a vampire because its skin was soft, like that of a living person, and its lips were rosy red.

Arnold drove a stake through the heart of the vampire and then cut off its head. Finally, Arnold burned the body and head until they were ashes.

When he had done what was necessary, Arnold quit the army and went home to the small Yugoslavian village where he had grown up.

Two years later, Arnold was killed when he fell from a hay wagon. He was buried in the church cemetery.

A month after Arnold's death, people began to report that they had seen him wandering around the village at night. Some said he came into their houses and when he left, they felt weak. Soon, people began to die, and the whole village panicked.

Everyone hung garlands of garlic on their windows and doors. But rumors spread that vampires could change into mist and slide under doors in the dead of night. No one was safe.

The village people called the government for help, and one morning a committee of three doctors, two soldiers, and a drummer boy went with city officials to dig up Arnold's body. When the coffin was opened, there was Arnold, looking fresh as a brand-new corpse. His eyes were open, his lips were red, and blood dripped down his cheek.

Arnold had been dead for three months, yet he looked as though he had died yesterday. There was no doubt in anyone's mind: Arnold was a vampire.

The committee sprinkled garlic into the coffin and then they drove a wooden stake through the vampire's heart.

Later, the report they filed said that when the stake went into the body, there was a terrifying shriek and the wound spurted blood.

The drummer boy fainted.

Next, the vampire's head was cut off and everything was burned. But still, the committee wasn't finished.

People continued to complain that there were vampires roaming the village. So all of Arnold's victims had to be dug up and "killed," too.

When it was all over, thirteen bodies had been reduced to ashes, and a major vampire "epidemic" had been averted.

On Becoming a Vampire:
Being Bitten

In vampire lore it's generally believed that victims of a vampire's bite automatically become vampires when they die. That's what causes vampire epidemics.

Let's say one vampire with a small appetite goes out some night and dines on one single victim, turning that victim into a vampire. The next night here are two vampires — and two victims. By the third night, that number has doubled again, creating four vampires and four victims. Here is a ten-day tally of vampires:

Night 1: 1 vampire — 1 victim
Night 2: 2 vampires — 2 victims
Night 3: 4 vampires — 4 victims
Night 4: 8 vampires — 8 victims
Night 5: 16 vampires — 16 victims
Night 6: 32 vampires — 32 victims
Night 7: 64 vampires — 64 victims
Night 8: 128 vampires — 128 victims
Night 9: 256 vampires — 256 victims
Night 10: 512 vampires — 512 victims

By the eleventh night, 1,024 vampires are roaming the countryside looking for dinner. And by the end of three weeks, there are 1,048,576 vampires!

It's said that the great vampire epidemic that spread through Central Europe from 1723 to 1735 created terror across the entire continent.

On Becoming a Vampire: Other Routes

Although being bitten by a vampire was believed to be the most common way of becoming a vampire, there were other routes as well.

According to some legends, liars and wicked people automatically became vampires.

Others thought that werewolves became vampires when they died, along with anyone who ate the flesh of a sheep that had been killed by a wolf.

And it was generally believed that the child of a werewolf and a vampire would become a vampire, also.

It was said in some cultures that a baby born with teeth was destined to become a vampire.

And so was the seventh son or daughter when all the children in the family were the same sex.

A murder victim was certain to become a vampire until the killer had been punished; and people who committed suicide were condemned to be vampires until the time came when they would have died naturally.

People cursed by their parents become vampires as well. There's an old Russian tale about a boy whose mother got angry one day. . . .

A Mother's Curse

"You're a wicked boy! I bring down my curse upon you!" screamed the enraged mother.

That night the child developed a terrible fever, and the next day he died.

For many, many long, horrible years, the village was tormented by the young vampire. Finally, just before she died, the mother was convinced to lift the curse on her son.

The old woman was taken to the cemetery, and the coffin was dug up. Sure enough, the corpse of the boy, like all vampire corpses, looked as if it were still alive.

While many of the townspeople watched, the ancient mother spoke. "I take back the curse I cast upon you," she croaked.

Instantaneously, in front of all their eyes, the boy's body crumbled into dust.

Trapping the Vampire

If people thought there was a possibility that a dead person might become a vampire, they had all sorts of methods of trapping the corpse in its coffin so she or he couldn't escape and make trouble. They would

- dig a very deep hole for the coffin.
- place heavy stones on top of the coffin.
- nail the corpse's skull into the wood of the coffin.

- hammer the corpse to the coffin with a wooden stake.
- chop off the head and the feet of the corpse.
- tie the big toes and thumbs together.
- bury the body with plenty of food so if the corpse got hungry, it wouldn't have to leave its grave.

Scaring the Vampire

It's said that a vampire was "strong as an ox and swift as the wind." But, according to the stories, there were some things vampires were afraid of.

They were terrified of holy items like crosses and crucifixes. So people put crosses into coffins; they folded the arms of a dead person to form a cross on his or her chest; and they sometimes buried a body at a place where two roads *crossed*.

Holy water was reputed to burn a vampire as if it were a biting acid. And communion wafers and pictures of saints were deadly to the unholy creature.

The people of Bulgaria used this fear of holy things in a very clever way. If a vampire was lurking in the neighborhood, a brave soul, holding a cross and a picture of a saint, went out to greet the creature. Since vampires ran away from such holy symbols, the person was able to chase the fleeing vampire right into a bottle. Of course, part of the trick involved putting the vampire's

13

favorite food — presumably blood — into the bottle beforehand.

When the monster went into the bottle to get his or her treat, the vampire-buster quickly corked the bottle and tossed it into a fire. That done, it's said that the vampire disappeared forever.

In addition to holy things, garlic has always been favored as a popular vampire-repellent. If a vampire was plaguing a town, the residents would hang garlic on their doors and windows. And, as added insurance against attack, many people wore garlic around their necks; for everyone was certain that vampires hated the smell of garlic.

In some countries people ate garlic for breakfast, lunch, and dinner, hoping that a vampire would find garlic-flavored blood disgusting.

And in Malaysia and China, people even rubbed garlic juice on their skin.

Brambles and thorns were also used as vampire-deterrents, for it was said that vampires were afraid their clothes might get caught in the sharp spikes and they'd be trapped and unable to return to their coffins by daylight. That's why Serbians and Bulgarians barricaded their doors and windows with thorny branches.

One strange Malaysian vampire was especially sensitive to thorns.

The Penangglan

From one area of Malaysia comes a strange and eerie legend. It seems a woman was being punished for some misdeed. Her punishment, apparently a common one at the time, was to sit, bent over, in a huge wooden barrel in the center of town. While she was in the barrel, a man came along and asked her why she was there.

Startled by his voice, the woman kicked her chin with such power that her head flew right off. Unfortunately, along with the head came her innards, and all of them floated away in the air.

Since that terrible time, this floating intestinal vampire has become known as the Penangglan.

The worst thing is that she feeds on the blood of innocent babies. It's said she enters people's homes through openings in the floorboards.

Understandably, wise Malaysians put the prickly branches of the Jenyu plant all over and under their houses, for the delicate, sensitive innards of the Penangglan cannot bear to pass through the prickles.

Avoiding Light

In most legends, vampires are allergic to daylight. Some stories say that if the creatures are caught in the light of day, they will instantly crumble into dust. Others report that the vampire who can't get back to its coffin on time simply falls over dead at dawn.

Lots of vampires have been undone by this allergy to daylight. Because of this, people devised a variety of ways to make the vampire stay out after dawn. For instance, in some countries it was said that vampires could not resist counting things. One very tricky way to keep a vampire from entering a house was to sprinkle thousands of tiny mustard seeds outside the house. If vampires happened to come along, they would be compelled to stop and count the seeds. And, if there were enough seeds, the vampires would still be counting at daybreak, when they would have to race back to their coffins . . . or crumble.

The Chinese believed that hiding the lid of the coffin after the vampire has left its grave would cause the returning vampire to crumble into dust.

And finally, there's the tale of . . .

The Rooster That Crowed at Night

Once long ago, in a small Russian city, there lived a man who was hated by everyone. He was a liar and a cheater; he was dishonest in business and cruel to his friends. When he died, nobody mourned him. His body lay alone in the church.

As was the custom in such situations, the caretaker of the church was asked to stay with the body all night and say prayers over it.

Now it was common knowledge that evil people often turn into vampires when they die. And that made the caretaker very nervous. So when he arrived at church late that afternoon, he carried a rooster under his arm.

All afternoon and evening the caretaker was alone with the corpse. Then, at midnight, while the caretaker was praying, the dead man suddenly jumped out of his coffin. Fangs bared and ready to bite, the vampire corpse rushed toward the caretaker.

As the vampire lunged, the caretaker reached down and pinched the rooster.

The rooster, shocked from his peaceful sleep, suddenly crowed.

And . . . thinking the cock's crow announced the arrival of morning, without a word the dead man dropped dead.

Finding the Right Grave

If a vampire couldn't be killed any other way, the body would be dug up during the day while she or he was sleeping. Then it could be properly eradicated. But in a cemetery full of graves, it wasn't always easy to know which grave belonged to the vampire.

Many years ago, the Hungarians devised an unusual but effective method for finding a vampire's grave. The first thing they did was choose a young boy who had never had a girlfriend. Then they put the boy on a coal-black stallion that had never stumbled.

The horse was ridden by the boy in and out among the graves. When the horse stopped at a grave and would not move even when it was whipped, that grave was certain to be the home of a vampire.

Another less complicated method for identifying the home of a vampire was to look for a grave that had four or five small holes in the dirt. These breathing holes were about the width of a man's finger and were a certain sign that a vampire lay below.

So say the legends.

Identifying a Vampire

Once a corpse was properly located and dug up, it was easy to figure out if it was a vampire. For a vampire corpse doesn't look dead at all; it looks like a sleeping person, often with a reddish face and a plump body.

Vampire expert Montague Summers describes it this way:

Sometimes the eyes are closed; more frequently open, glazed, fixed and glaring fiercely. The lips which will be markedly full and red are drawn back from the teeth which gleem long, sharp, as razors, and ivory white. Often the gaping mouth is stained and foul with great slab gouts of blood, which trickles down from the corners.

Killing the Dead

Once the vampire was found, it had to be "killed." The most common method was to drive a wooden stake through its body with only one blow. It was widely believed that a second or third blow might wake up the vampire and bring it back to life.

One vampire in Bohemia who was killed with multiple blows was said to have thanked the man who drove the stake through his heart.

"I'll use the stake as a club to keep away the dogs," he said genially.

Another vampire is said to have pulled the stake out of his heart and thrown it back at the horrified executioner.

In a method that definitely smacked of overkill, once the vampire had been "staked," its head had to be cut off with a gravedigger's shovel. Some legends even advised stuffing the mouth with garlic before chopping.

And finally, as if all this stabbing and chopping and stuffing weren't enough, everything in the coffin — including the vampire's body — had to be burned to ashes. This had to be done carefully, however. For, according to vampire expert Summers, "Any animals which may come forth from the fire — worms, snakes, lice, beetles, birds of horrible and deformed shape — must be driven back into the flames, for it may be that the Vampire [is] embodied in one of these, seeking escape so that he can renew his foul parasitism of death."

Finding Alternatives

Clearly, over the years there have been lots of people who favored less gruesome ways to get rid of a vampire.

Those with delicate sensibilities preferred to kill their vampires by shooting them with a silver bullet that had been blessed by a priest. But once they had a dead vampire, these people had to be careful not to lay the corpse in the rays of the moonlight, especially if the moon was full. For vampires killed by a silver bullet are brought back to life by moonlight, and they resume their gory activities with greater strength and even more malevolence.

Or so the legends say.

There are, of course, many other vampire-extermination methods. Some legends promote a sort of gourmet cooking route, claiming that boiling the vampire's heart in vinegar and oil is effective. Others favor cutting up the body and boiling it in wine.

In an effort to avoid such gory procedures, the people in one part of Greece merely transported the corpse of a vampire to an uninhabited island and buried it with all the other vampires. Vampires, it was said, were unable to cross salt water.

Tricking the Vampire

Vampires were apparently not all that smart, for there are lots of stories where they are tricked to their death. The bottle story and the mustard-seed story are two of them. Here's a third.

The Vampire in the Clock Tower

For more than three years, a small village in Moravia was plagued by a vampire. With each month the terror grew worse, until people were afraid to go out at night. Even when they were locked in their homes they were frightened, for somehow this vampire didn't seem to be scared away by garlic or crosses or even thorny branches.

At the peak of the terror, a man from the neighboring country of Hungary passed through town. A gentleman with considerable experience in vampire eradication, he offered to help.

Late that afternoon the man climbed up the clock tower of the church. From there, he had a good view of the cemetery below.

Soon after sunset, the resident vampire rose from his grave. He looked around to make certain he was safe. Then he shed his body wrappings, leaving the soiled winding-sheet in his blood-befouled coffin. Hungry and thirsty, the vampire made his way into the village to terrorize people.

As soon as the hideous monster was out of sight, the Hungarian exterminator climbed down from the church tower and crept into the cemetery. There, he stole the long sheet that the vampire had been buried in.

Later that night when the vampire returned, he discovered that his sheet was missing. Screaming in rage and distress at having been robbed of his covering, the vampire happened to look up at the church tower. There was the Hungarian, waving the sheet like a demented bullfighter and calling the vampire to come get it.

Enraged, the vampire started up the stairs. But the Hungarian was waiting for him. Without any warning, the man hit the vampire over the head, knocked him out, and then chopped off his head with a gravedigger's shovel.

And, says the report, "that made an end of the whole business."

Dracula and Vlad the Impaler

The most famous vampire of all is a character named Count Dracula from a book of the same name by Bram Stoker. It was written in 1897.

In the book, Dracula was a nobleman who lived in a castle in Transylvania (then a province of Hungary; today a part of Romania). He slept by day in a coffin and only went out at night.

Sometimes Count Dracula was a charming gentleman. Other times he was a blood-sucking vampire who could turn himself into a bat in order to kill his friends and suck their blood.

In the movie *Dracula*, starring Bela Lugosi, Bram Stoker's Dracula character was tall and lean and pale. He wore a long black cape and spoke with a foreign accent. Ever since the movie came out in 1931, Lugosi's Dracula has been everybody's picture of what a real vampire was supposed to be.

However, in the most recent vampire movies, the vampires are more or less ordinary people, just as they are in the legends.

The original Dracula has also been the inspiration for cereal (Count Chocula); candy (Count Crunch); and television characters such as the Count on *Sesame Street* and Count Duckula, a cartoon character who is mistakenly transfused with ketchup instead of blood and gets uncontrollable urges for broccoli.

In England there was an ice-cream bar called Count Dracula's Deadly Secret — Eat One Before Sunset. The ice cream was "moon white," and the coating was "black-as-night."

There are also Dracula-inspired greeting cards:

- "It's Halloween. And you look good enough to eat."
- "Do I vish you a vonderful Halloween? You bat I do."

And riddles:

- "What is Dracula's favorite holiday?"
  "Fangsgiving."

- "What kind of a dog does Dracula have?"
  "A bloodhound."

- "Where did they put Dracula when he was arrested?"
  "In a red blood cell."

It's because of the Dracula movie that people think vampires talk with a foreign accent, as in, "I vant to suck your blood." In the original movie, Lugosi speaks with an accent . . . and forever after people who pretend to be vampires have also spoken with an accent.

Bram Stoker, the writer of the book, got the name Dracula from a real person who lived near Transylvania in the 1400s. The real Dracula wasn't a count; he was a prince. And he wasn't a vampire, either. Actually, he was worse than any vampire.

As people go, Vlad Tepes, also known as Prince Dracula, was about as horrible as you can get.

Dracula means Little Dragon or Little Devil. There's no question that Dracula lived up to his name.

During his years as the ruler of the kingdom of Walachia, Prince Dracula became known as one of the cruelest torturers ever known.

One time, some soldiers from another country made the horrible mistake of trespassing onto Dracula's land. Fiercely annoyed at this intrusion, the Prince ordered three of the soldiers to be fried in oil. Then he forced the other soldiers to eat their comrades. While they were eating, Prince Dracula told the surviving soldiers that if they did not join his army, they would have to eat each other until there was only one man left.

They joined.

Dracula was also a vindictive enemy. When he won a battle, he punished the losers by skewering them on poles and leaving them to squirm until they died. It's said that after one battle, he had 20,000 soldiers impaled on stakes.

Another time Prince Dracula invited some friends to dinner. All around the table, decaying bodies were impaled on the tops of sticks. One of the guests was foolish enough to complain that the stink was terrible. Vlad solved the guest's problem by having the poor man impaled on a pole of his own, taller than all the others so he wouldn't be troubled by the smell.

In all, it's said that Prince Dracula impaled some 100,000 people.

Although Stoker preferred to use his nickname, history remembers Dracula as Vlad the Impaler. Whatever the name — Prince Dracula or Vlad the Impaler — there's no doubt he was a fitting inspiration for the most famous vampire story of all.

Variations on the Vampire

Not all vampires are the same. Different cultures create different stories of vampires. The following story is from the folk lore of Armenia.

A Tale Told from the Sole

Long ago, on a huge mountain in Armenia, there dwelled an unusual kind of vampire named Dakhanavar. He lived in a cave instead of a grave, and when he sucked the blood of his victims, he did it through the soles of their feet.

Dakhanavar considered the mountain his personal property; he couldn't stand it when people wandered in to enjoy its beauty. And he became especially enraged when they tried to count the valleys around it. He considered them *his* valleys, and it was nobody's business to count them. Whenever people came along and started counting, Dakhanavar visited them at night and sucked their blood from the soles of their feet until they died.

Now it happened that one day two clever young men came into Dakhanavar's territory and started to count the valleys. When they finished their first day's counting, the two men lay down to go to sleep. They had heard of Dakhanavar's night-thirst, so before they slept, each carefully put his feet underneath the head of the other.

When Dakhanavar arrived in the dark, he leaned over and touched a head. Then, he felt his way down to where the feet were supposed to be. But instead of feet, he found another head.

"Aaah!" Dakhanavar screeched. "I have traveled the whole of these 366 valleys and I have sucked the blood of hundreds of people, but never before have I found a person with two heads and no feet!"

And with that, he began running until he was off the mountain, through the village, and out of the country, never to be seen again. And what's more, everyone from that day on knew that the mountain had 366 valleys.

* * *

A final vampirelike creature that is part of the folklore of Japan is called a kappa. Kappas are not the dead who have come back to life, but they do suck blood like vampires.

Kappas are green, about the size of a ten-year-old boy, and on the tops of their heads is a hollow, filled with water. If a kappa loses the water in his head, he loses his power.

Kappas lived in rivers and lakes and lure people and animals into the water so they can suck their blood.

Fortunately, kappas like to eat cucumbers as well. Superstitious people who live near a river carve the names of their family on cucumbers and throw them into the water. The kappas eat the cucumbers and leave the people alone.

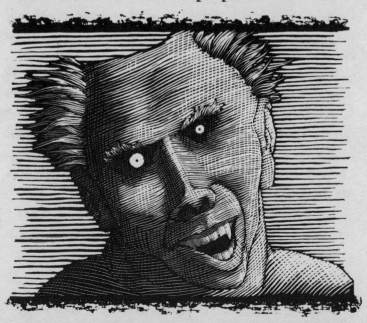

Believing in Vampires

So, as you can see, there are almost as many different stories of different kinds of vampires as there are places in the world. Some are green; some are furry; some have eyes that are fiery red. But no matter how they differed, whatever language they spoke, all vampires were believed to have an insatiable lust for human blood.

Strange, don't you think, that such totally different cultures have all given life to the same "imaginary" character?

Werewolves

"Mommy, am I a werewolf?"
"Shut up and comb your face."

•

Werewolf mother to werewolf child: "How many times have I told you not to speak with someone in your mouth?"

•

Little Willie ate his sister
She was dead before we missed her.
Willie's always up to tricks.
Ain't he cute.
He's only six.
— *By anonymous werewolf*

According to the Legends

A werewolf is someone who's capable of changing from a perfectly regular person into a ferocious wolf.

During the day, most werewolves appear to be ordinary people. But at night, especially during the full moon, these *ordinary people* turn into wolves.

The transformed wolves are said to be bigger and faster and stronger than regular wolves. And smarter as well. For werewolves have the strength and instincts of an animal . . . and the brains of a human.

In some werewolf tales, the animals travel on two feet. But in most they move on four. In their animal form, werewolves rampage through villages in search of sheep and cattle and goats to eat. They also find people quite tasty, and are said to be particularly fond of children.

Identifying Werewolves
When They Are People

Werewolves are called *shape-shifters* because they can change the shape of their bodies from one form (human) to another (wolf).

When they are people, they look like . . . well, look around. Any of the people you see could be werewolves. According to the legends, they are old and young, male and female, rich and poor. Some tales even talk about baby werewolves.

Although most werewolves can't be detected when they're in their human mode, it's said that there are some who, as humans, have hairy palms, extremely penetrating eyes, and eyebrows that meet in the middle above their noses. And occasionally, even in their human form, some werewolves have clawlike nails, especially long canine teeth, and a pronounced fondness for raw meat.

Another way of identifying a werewolf while in its human form is by the wounds on its body. Any injury inflicted upon a werewolf when she or he is a wolf is certain to show up later on the human's body. There are many werewolf stories in which severed legs, knife wounds, and decapitations (chopped-off heads) show up on the human, even though the injuries were inflicted upon the wolf.

Even scratches and bruises that the wolf gets from running through thorny bushes also appear on the person.

Usually, though, werewolves are ordinary people until they are beckoned by the bright light of the full moon. Then, drawn by blood-lust and an irresistable urge, those *ordinary people* climb out bedroom windows, sneak out back doors, and hide in dark alleys where they abandon their humanness and give life to the dark wolf-nature within them.

So say the legends.

Identifying Werewolves
When They Are Wolves

In wolf form, werewolves are ferocious and terrifying. They howl an eerie, mystical call that travels for miles across the boundaries of the night.

This terrible noise is matched by an awesome appearance. Werewolves are not only larger and stronger and meaner than regular wolves, they have sharp, cruel teeth, mighty paws, and supernatural speed as well.

Most stories suggest that the werewolf has a human intelligence enabling it to plot its attacks and trick its victims. And some stories claim that the beast can cast magic spells on bullets.

As in all myths and legends, the werewolf varies from place to place. But one trait is nearly universal: Werewolves have a craving for the sweet, delicate taste of beautiful women, and the delicious, fresh flavor of children's brains.

Hunting the Werewolf

There are lots of werewolf stories in the world. Some are made up by modern writers. And some were probably made up by ancient writers and storytellers.

But there are also tales told by peasants, farmers, hunters — simple people, frightened people. These stories have been collected by "werewolf scholars." "A Hairy Tale" is one of those.

A Hairy Tale

Over four hundred years ago, near a village in western France, a gentleman lived with his beautiful wife in a small castle. In the evening when the mist drifted over the meadow, they liked to sit quietly together and gaze out the window. There the couple watched the road that ran past the castle.

One day a hunter and his dog passed by.

"Where are you going?" called the gentleman to his friend.

"To the forest," replied the hunter. "I've heard tales of a strange wolf living there."

"Sometimes I hear the terrible howls at night. Perhaps it's the same wolf."

Just then the dog looked up at the window and began to growl.

"Strange," said the hunter. "This is a hunting dog. She only growls at animals."

The gentleman's wife smiled nervously as the dog's fangs glinted sharp and hungry in the moonlight.

"Your dog is eager for the hunt," said the gentleman. "Go now. Stop by to see me when you return."

"I'll do that," said the friend. "I should return by midnight."

The forest was dark, but the moon was full. Eerie shadows danced crazily on the forest floor.

Unafraid, the hunter walked with his dog deeper and deeper into the woods.

Suddenly the howl of a lone wolf tore through the silence of the night.

The hunter stopped, pointing his gun toward the noise. The hairs on the dog's back stood up as it caught the familiar scent of danger.

Standing very still, the hunter waited quietly for another sign from the wolf.

Crash! Without a moment's warning, a gigantic wolf bolted from the bushes and leapt at the startled hunter.

Bang! The hunter squeezed the trigger of his gun, but the bullet missed its mark.

Frantic, the dog jumped toward the wolf. With one sweep of its huge paw, the wolf flung the dog aside.

Gripping his knife, the hunter swung the sharp blade blindly toward the animal. With a single, desperate cut, the knife severed the wolf's paw.

Screeching and howling in pain, the wolf ran bleeding into the dark safety of the forest.

I've never seen a wolf so fierce, thought the hunter as he leaned over and looked at the bloody, severed paw that lay on the ground. As proof of his deadly encounter, he picked up the paw, wrapped it in a cloth, and put it in his knapsack. Then he and his dog walked wearily back to the castle.

"So did you find the wolf?" asked the gentleman as he welcomed his friend to the castle.

"It was the most ferocious animal I've ever seen," said the hunter. Then he proceeded to tell the gentleman what happened. To prove his tale, he pulled the bloody package from his knapsack. Slowly, he unwound the cloth from the paw.

"What is this!" cried the gentleman in horror. "That isn't a wolf's paw. It's the hand of a lady!"

"Ah!" cried the hunter. "What have I done?"

"The ring!" said the gentleman. "I know that ring! It belongs to my wife!"

The man hurried to his wife's room and ran to the bed where she lay. Throwing back the covers, he screamed in horror when he saw the bloody stump where once there had been a hand.

Becoming a Werewolf on Purpose

It's not all that clear why anyone would actually *want* to become a werewolf. But over the years and throughout the world, people have devised methods for achieving this dubious goal.

According to legends, if you wanted to become a werewolf, you could

- eat the brains of a wolf.
- drink from a stream where wolves drink.
- pick a magic flower that grows in the mountains of the Balkans.
- drink water from a wolf's footprint.
- wear a magical wolfskin belt.
- cover your body with magic salve and wear the whole skin of a wolf.
- sleep with the light of the moon shining on your face on a Wednesday or Friday night in the summer when the moon is full.

One rather complicated method involved the would-be werewolf climbing to the top of a hill during a full moon. At midnight, he or she had to draw two circles on the ground, one inside the

other. The first circle had to be three feet across. The second, seven feet.

Next, she or he had to build a fire and over it hang an iron pot from an iron tripod. The pot then had to be filled with water and a secret mixture of herbs.

Once the magic potion was boiling, the would-be werewolf was supposed to kneel in the space between the two circles and sing a special song. (Care had to be taken *never* to kneel inside the small circle. If that mistake was made, the potential werewolf risked being snatched away by evil spirits.)

After all this was done, the near-wolf had to smear a magic salve all over her or his body, put on a wolfskin, and wait for the transformation.

Becoming a Werewolf by Accident

It may seem odd to feel sorry for werewolves, but some of these creatures were very sad individuals. They didn't *want* to be werewolves; it just happened.

These "accidental" werewolves knew they couldn't risk telling people what they were or they would have been thrown in jail . . . or worse. They couldn't even tell their friends or family; it's not exactly the kind of information people can accept casually. Above all, these "accidental" werewolves hated the fact that they were compelled, when the moon was full, to commit horrible, bloody acts.

Sometimes when they felt an attack coming on, "accidental" werewolves had themselves locked into special rooms that had bars on the windows and doors. There, tormented and alone, they spent the night trying to escape. These people usually left instructions that no matter what happened — no matter how furiously they screamed or how pitifully they begged — the door must not be opened until morning.

There are other stories of werewolves, desperate to deny the powerful call of the full moon, who strapped themselves to the bed when they felt an attack coming on.

Fortunately, accidental transformations were rare. But they did happen. Or so say the legends.

It was said that some people accidentally drank from a magic mountain stream that turned them into terrifying beasts.

Others might have innocently picked a magic flower. Some legends say that the blossom looks like a red daisy. Others say it's similar to a white sunflower. And still others say it's like a yellow snapdragon.

In many countries people believed that a person who survived the bite of a werewolf would surely turn into one.

And some legends even claimed that if you were a werewolf in life, you were destined to be a vampire after death. That's called a no-win situation.

Believing in Werewolves

Did people really believe in werewolves? Some did. The following tale is an example of just how strong that belief could be.

"I can't imagine why it happens."

A long time ago — so long ago that the date and place have been lost — a thief was hanging around a small country inn, looking for something to steal. Three days went by, and he didn't even come across one scrawny chicken to make his own.

By the fourth day the thief was ready to give up and move on when a man strolled out of the inn and sat down on a bench.

The first thing the thief noticed was that the man was wearing a magnificent cape. Lined with fur and made of the finest wool, this was, indeed, a cape fit for a king.

The thief glanced around. No one else was in sight, so he casually sat down next to the man. For a while, the two men made small talk about the inn, the weather, and other inconsequential things.

After a few minutes, the thief yawned, opening his mouth very wide. Then he leaned his head back and howled.

Startled, the man looked at the thief and asked, "What's the matter?"

"I might as well tell you," said the thief, "for you'll know soon enough. You see, I have this problem. I don't know why, but every once in a while, I'm seized with the need to lean back and yawn and howl. Maybe I'm being punished for my sins."

Then the thief yawned again, opening his jaws even wider. "Ouwwwww!" he howled. "OuwwwwOuwww!"

Trying not to appear rude, the poor man scooted to the end of the bench.

"I can't imagine why it happens," said the thief with an innocent smile as he moved closer to the stranger. "But after I've yawned three times, just like that, presto! I turn into a huge wolf — one of those horrible beasts that gobbles up people in a trice, bones and all."

Now that man was no fool. Not wasting any time, he jumped up and tried to run, but the clever thief grabbed the man's cape.

"Don't go yet," said the thief, still clutching the cape. "Wait a minute, and I'll give you my clothes to hold. I don't want to lose them." As he spoke, he yawned again, opening his mouth so wide he nearly cracked his jaw.

The terrified man — not at all interested in becoming dinner for a werewolf — slipped out of his cape and ran through the door of the inn, bolting it securely behind him. He didn't wait to hear the thief howl for the third time.

As for the thief, he wrapped himself up in his fine, new cape and set off to see more of the world.

Dewolfing

It isn't difficult to understand why the poor gentleman ran from the thief. There are probably plenty of us today who would run if we met such a man . . . especially if it happened at night.

Given the strength of werewolf fears that flourished in Europe and Asia during the seventeenth and eighteenth centuries, it's understandable that a belief system would grow about how to get rid of the curse of werewolfism.

Getting rid of the terrible beasts was not only difficult, but a bit of a dilemma as well. For werewolves were beastly only part of the time — when they were in their wolf state. When they were people, they were quite ordinary. The problem was that if you killed the wolf, who *was* dangerous, you also killed the person, who wasn't. So killing the monster was considered a bit harsh.

Experts told of other methods. First, they suggested that the werewolf hunter be absolutely certain the suspect really was a werewolf. The most common way to do that was to wait for a full moon and then follow the person suspected of being a werewolf. If this person ran off naked into the countryside to terrorize the population, it was a pretty good bet that she or he was a werewolf.

It was easy at that point to steal the clothes the werewolf left behind and prevent him — or her — from becoming human again. But the result of this action was the opposite of what was desired. Instead of getting rid of the werewolf, this method got rid of the person. And the town would then be stuck with a permanent werewolf.

A better method of werewolf eradication was to catch the wolf and tie it up. Then, according to an ancient formula, the wolf must be cut three times on the forehead with a knife. After that the beast could be set free. When she — or he — became a human again, the curse would be gone.

And finally, according to some stories, perhaps

the easiest way to get rid of the wolf side of a werewolf was to throw a piece of clothing at it. They say that an apron or even a shirt would often do the trick.

There's a story from Denmark of a man who hated being a werewolf. . . .

The Apron Method

There once was a young man named Peter who went with his bride for a ride in his carriage one night when the moon was full. Suddenly, a terrible and familiar sensation coursed through his body . . . and he knew he was turning into a werewolf.

Horrified, Peter jumped from the carriage and told his wife to travel on.

"And should anything come out of the woods to attack you," he cautioned, "don't be frightened. And don't hurt it."

"What should I do?"

"Hit it with your apron," said Peter.

A few minutes later, a huge wolf leapt out of the forest and growled at the beautiful young bride. Remembering what she had been told, she ripped off her apron and swung it at the wolf's face.

Instead of attacking her, the wolf grabbed the apron and ran away.

A few minutes later, Peter came out of the woods with the apron in his hand.

The young bride cried out when she saw him. "I can't believe I'm married to a werewolf!"

"You were," Peter said to her. "But now the curse has been lifted."

In the interest of safety, it should be noted that there are those who doubt the effectiveness of a flimsy piece of fabric thrown in the face of a snarling beast.

Escaping the Werewolf

Long ago, in the event of a werewolf attack, there wasn't much anyone could do except yell good-bye.

It was rumored, however, that if the victim happened to be within a short distance of an ash tree, and could manage to climb it, the magic of the ash would keep the werewolf away.

And some experts also claimed that were-wolves could not enter a field of rye.

The unfortunate part of this solution is that it's highly unlikely that a person about to be de-voured by a werewolf would just happen to be wandering around near a ryefield . . . or an ash tree.

Asking Why

There's no doubt that people believed humans could change themselves into wolves. For the Western mind, that's certainly a strange thought.

But the idea has been around for hundreds of years.

"Were" comes from "wer," which meant "man" in Old English. So if you put the two words together, "werewolf" means man-wolf.

Although there are lots of theories about the origin of wereanimals, no one will ever know for sure where they all began.

There are many religions — especially in Asia and Africa — in which it is believed the human spirit can enter an animal. And most religions believe the human being has a soul that's separate from the body. Given these beliefs, it's really not so strange that people might think a wolf could have a human soul inside it.

But the idea of humans actually turning into animals is another thing altogether. Perhaps the belief is based on the suspicion that we all have an animal lurking within us.

Or perhaps the idea had its origins in certain rare physical and psychological conditions that may have led people to believe that humans could become animallike, both in behavior and appearance. One of those conditions is a mental disorder called lycanthropy, which also means "man-wolf."

Lycanthropy is a mental illness that causes people to believe they are wolves. They behave in frightening, animalistic ways — especially during the full moon — sometimes even howling and running around on four "feet." People who suffer from this delusion often become violent and act like the legendary werewolves. They don't actually change their shape, but in some cases they do wear the skin of a wolf during the time they're trapped in their violent behavior. The following story was probably a case of lycanthropy.

The Teenage Werewolf

It happened in the year 1603 in southwest France. Young children were disappearing without a trace. Once, even a baby was stolen from its cradle while the mother went into the other room to fetch a sweater.

Some people said that wolves caused these strange disappearances. Others said it was worse than wolves.

Then a thirteen-year-old girl swore that one night when the moon was full, she had been attacked by a beast that looked like a wolf.

"I was watching the cattle," she said, "when a wild, furry beast rushed from the bushes and tore my clothing. I was only able to save myself by poking the beast with an iron-pointed staff."

Then another girl, this one eighteen, claimed to have spoken to Jean Grenier, a thirteen-year-old young man who lived at the edge of town.

"Grenier confessed to me that he's a werewolf," claimed the young woman. "And he says he frequently puts on a magical wolfskin and rampages like a crazed beast through fields and woods." Then she added something even worse. "Grenier told me he often craves the flesh of tender, plump children."

In his definitive book on werewolves, Montague Summers writes that Grenier "had often killed dogs and lapped their hot blood, which was not so delicious to his taste as that of young boys, from whose thighs he would bite great collops of fat luscious brawn."

Eventually, Grenier was caught and brought to trial. He confessed that he had been a werewolf, and that all the gruesome things that were said about him by parents of missing children were true.

Because he was so young, Grenier was not killed. Instead, he was ordered to go live in a monastery. Some years after he had been sent away, a researcher went to see him. Summers reports the following account:

> . . . he was a lean and gaunt lad, with small deep-set eyes that glared fiercely. He had long, sharp teeth, some of which were white like fangs, others black and broken, whilst his hands were almost like claws with horrid crooked nails. He loved to hear and talk of wolves, often fell upon all fours, moving with extraordinary agility and seemingly with greater

ease than when he walked upright as a man.

There are also some other rare conditions that may have once given people the "proof" that shape-shifting was possible. In one, a disease called porphyria, the infected person's skin is harmed by sunlight. As a consequence, the person can only venture from his or her home at night. People afflicted with this disease also become physically disfigured and mentally deranged. It stands to reason that a disfigured person who avoids the sun, goes out only at night, and behaves in crazy ways might be mistaken for a werewolf.

And finally, there is another disease, so rare that in all of history there have only been a few cases. But the disease is so odd that tales of those few cases probably spread widely throughout the population. The disease, called *Hypertrichosia universalis congenita*, causes a person to grow hair from four to ten inches long, all over his or her body. The hair is fine, like that of an Angora cat . . . and the only places it doesn't grow are on the bottoms of hands and feet, on the lips, and at the ends of fingers and toes.

Certainly tales of such hairy humans could have given people images of shape-shifting. And in cultures that did not yet have psychological or scientific explanations for human abnormalities, it was not so absurd to conjure up werewolves.

Variations on the Werewolf

All over the world, shape-shifting tales have been told. In Europe, where wolves once thrived in dense forests, people allegedly turned into werewolves. In countries where there were fewer or no wolves, people turned into other animals. For instance, in Russia there are tales of werebears. In Africa, there are wereleopards, werelions, and werehyenas. And in South America, there are werejaguars.

It's said that, in Japan, people used to be so frightened of the werefox that in order to protect themselves from this dreaded creature, they carried the foot of a turtle in their left hand at all times.

And in India, there's a story about . . .

A Weretiger Named Baba

Baba had no trouble changing into a tiger. Basically it just happened when the time was right.

But in order to become human again, Baba needed a friend; someone who would stand in front of the tiger and say some magic words. After weretiger Baba spent a night or two ravaging the countryside, he would run to his best friend, Ali, and Ali would say the magic words that would transform his friend back into human form.

Unfortunately, one day Ali suddenly died. Baba grieved deeply for the loss of his best friend. He also grieved because he knew the next time he turned himself into a tiger, there would be no way for him to resume human form once more.

Baba thought about this problem for a long time. He had no other friends he could trust with the knowledge that he was a weretiger.

Finally, in desperation, Baba went to his wife. She was a nice enough woman, but she wasn't very smart.

"I have a big problem," he said to her.

When she heard the serious tone of his voice, she knew he was going to tell her something important.

"Every month during the full moon I get the urge to become a tiger," Baba said.

"But you always go to the city during the full moon," said his wife.

"No . . ." said Baba. "The truth is, I change into a weretiger. And the only way I can become human again is if someone says some magic words to me. Until Ali died, he was the one who said the words. Now I need you to do it for me."

After she recovered from the shock of learning she was married to a weretiger, Baba's wife agreed to say the magic words when he appeared to her in the form of a tiger.

Much relieved, Baba waited until the next full moon and then changed himself into a tiger. After he had eaten a couple of people and terrorized the countryside for a few days, he decided he wanted to become human once more.

So that night, he approached his wife when she was in the kitchen.

"Aarghhh!" she cried when she saw the huge tiger standing in the doorway. And she ran screaming out into the dark.

For three nights Baba approached his wife, hoping she would remember to say the magic words. And three times she became so frightened that she forgot to do it.

The fourth night Baba tried again. And again his wife ran away.

Baba was furious! He grew so angry at his

wife for being stupid that he attacked her and ate her up. It wasn't until after he finished his dinner that Baba realized that his wife wasn't the only stupid person in the family.

One Last Tale

Many of the werewolf tales in this book are retold from ancient documents, village records, and oral reports that were often collected years after they had happened. The following story took place in ancient Rome. In his book on werewolves, Montague Summers tells us it's one of the first werewolf stories ever recorded.

"Excuse me a minute."

Niceros was going to visit a friend. Since the friend lived far away and Niceros was traveling at night, he convinced a young soldier he knew to keep him company on the long journey.

The full moon was shining as brightly as the sun, and just as they were passing a cemetery, the soldier excused himself and went into the graveyard. Niceros thought the soldier had gone off to go to the bathroom in private.

"So, I sat me down singing away to myself and counting the stars overhead.

"After a while I looked round to see what my companion was up to, and ecod! my heart jumped into my very mouth. He had taken off all his clothes and laid them in a heap by the road's edge.

"I tell you I was as dumped as a dead man, for I saw him . . . [marking] in a circle all around his clothes, and then hey presto! he turned into a wolf.

"Please don't think I'm joking; I wouldn't tell a lie, no, not for a mint of money. But as I was just saying, in a trice he turned into a wolf, and thereupon he began to howl horribly and ran off full tilt into the woods.

"I didn't know whether I was standing on my head or my heels, and when I went to gather up his clothes, why they had all been changed into stone! Frightened! Phew! I was half-dead with fear."

Niceros continued on to his friend's house. Immediately upon his arrival, Niceros discovered that a huge wolf had just whipped through the yard, eating sheep and causing havoc.

"Master Wolf didn't get off scot free all the same," said Niceros' friend, "for our man gave him a good jab across the neck with a pike."

Poor Niceros was terrified. So as soon as daylight arrived, he rushed back to the place where his friend had left the clothes the night before.

"I could see nothing but a horrid pool of blood!

"At last I reached home, and there I found my soldier abed, bleeding like an ox in the shambles, whilst the doctor was busy dressing a deep gash in his neck.

"Then I knew that he was a werewolf, and after that I could neither bite nor sup with him; no, not if you had killed me for it.

"Yes; you can all think what you like of my tale, but Heaven help me never! if I've told a word of a lie."

Finally . . .

It's clear there are many different ideas about how people came to believe in werewolves. It would be easy to just laugh at the foolishness of such silly tales and dismiss them as figments of bizarre imaginations.

On the other hand, there's got to be a reason why these strange tales have continued to persist throughout the ages. When all is said and done, we'll never really know how much fact and how much fantasy forms the foundation for the widespread belief in wereanimals.

Perhaps werewolf tales have endured because there's something enticing about having the power to become a strong, invincible beast that's feared by everyone and surpassed by few. Or perhaps those tales are still with us because we all have an animal within us.

Personal Monsters

Kid: "Help, Mom!
There's a monster in
my room."

Mom: "Go to sleep,
George. It's just your
imagination."

According to the Legend

As we said in the beginning of this book, there have always been scary beasts of the night. For as long as there have been people, there have been monsters to torment them. This is as true today as it was thousands of years ago.

Vampires and werewolves are *cultural* monsters created in myths and legends throughout the world. But there's another kind of night monster we forget about: A monster that can haunt our sunniest days as well as our darkest nights. The authors call these *personal* monsters and, alas, we know them well.

No matter how many years have passed, no matter how smart we are, how brave we are, or how old we are — we all have our monsters to conquer.

My Own Night Monsters
by Nancy Lamb

Some people I know claim they were never afraid of night monsters, even though they suspected one or two unpleasant creatures might be lurking under their bed. And, astonishingly, I even know some very lucky people who say they didn't have any monsters at all.

Unfortunately, that's not true of me.

For starters, when I was a child, a witch lived

in my closet at night. I knew she was there because sometimes I'd wake up when the room was shrouded in darkness and I could see her quite clearly — a black, ominous shape hovering in the closet. Sometimes she stood still. Other times she would start to move toward me. Either way, when I saw her I'd crawl under my covers in terror.

The witch wasn't the only thing that scared me. Every once in a while when the moon was full and the pale light in my room cast eerie shadows on the wall, I'd hear the whistle of a train far far away.

Oooohhhhh . . . Oooooooooo. . . .

When that happened, I absolutely believed that train whistle was the sound of Mother Goose coming to get me. She didn't fly on a goose, either. She flew on a broom-stick. Actually, this flying terror was sort of an all-purpose cross between the famous nursery rhyme figure and the Wicked Witch of the West.

I can't possibly imagine where I came up with such a preposterous idea. But on those nights when the light was right and the train whistle called from across town, I was convinced that Mother Goose Witch was real. And I was once again thrust into a state of silent dread.

By far the worst night monster I ever had was the Beast who lived under my bed.

As a small child, I was absolutely certain this Beast could reach up from the end of my bed, slide his terrible claws silently under the sheet, and grab my ankles. If this should ever happen, he would then pull me into the everlasting darkness beneath my bed where I would simply disappear forever.

Needless to say, the Bed Beast was no wimp. Not this one. I was so convinced this monster was real that I would never *ever* put my arms or legs over the side of the bed. And I certainly wouldn't even *consider* the possibility of standing next to my bed in the middle of the night.

That, of course, made the task of getting in and

out of bed in the dark a bit of a challenge. But I was up to it.

If I had to get out of bed in the middle of the night to go to the bathroom, I'd jump several feet away from the bed, thudding loudly onto the floor and scampering across the room. Somehow I knew my monster couldn't reach very far from the bed. And when I returned, I'd take a running, flying leap from almost the middle of the room. And I'd land squarely on top of the bed.

I'm happy to report I never missed. On the other hand, I'm not so happy to report that I once jumped on a friend who was spending the night.

As if that reaction to the Beast weren't bad enough, this fear of mine led me to an even greater extreme: I always slept on my side with my legs doubled up. Trust me. There wasn't enough money in the world to make me straighten out my legs, because that would allow the Beast to grab my ankles.

Now, when you sleep doubled up for hours on end, you're bound to get leg cramps. I would often awaken in the middle of the night with terrible pains in my legs. My mother would come to comfort me, to massage the cramps away. And yet I never once told her about the Beast under my bed who was the cause of all my grief.

I suppose I thought she wouldn't understand; that she'd just dismiss my fears by saying all the monsters were figments of my very active imagination. It never occurred to me that when my mother was a little girl, she probably had her own set of horrible night-haunting monsters.

And with all my experience in dreaded night monsters, just the other day when I was talking to my twenty-one-year-old son, I asked if he had any creatures living in the dark of his room when he was little.

"Sure," he said. "I had lots of them. But I was afraid to tell you because I didn't think you'd understand."

Other People's Monsters
by Rita Golden Gelman

Okay. So I'm one of those unimaginative people whose night monsters aren't the least bit interesting. Not that I didn't have a few; it's just that they didn't have names or faces or shapes. And I didn't live in terror that they'd "get" me.

I did have the feeling that there might be *something* in my closet — something mildly scary — and I always made sure that the closet door was shut when I went to sleep. I still do. And as for the guys under the bed, well, I thought about them now and then; and I *always* kept a sheet over me for protection. But I didn't leap from the middle of the floor or cramp up every night.

A part of me sits here, as an adult, wishing I had some juicy monsters to talk about. And another part of me, the part that has been listening to friends talk about how they lived in terror for much of their childhood, is thankful. I don't know why some people have monsters and others don't. Maybe I was spared because I shared the room with my brother and it wasn't as scary as sleeping in a room alone.

Anyway, since I didn't have my own monsters, I've decided to report on other people's.

A ten-year-old girl named Genevieve says sometimes she wakes up in the middle of the night and ET is hiding behind her curtain. And it's not a nice ET, either. He's "scary and mean and very creepy. I just lie there scared with the sheet pulled up to my chin."

And my friend Ben has a lion named Merge that lives in his closet. "Merge is just medium-scary," Ben says. "I can protect myself from him by staying covered with my blanket."

A friend named Noah lived in terror of the Watermelon Baby when he was a child.

"I was only about four years old when I learned about the Watermelon Baby. This big kid told me all about him, and somehow I actually started to believe that this hideous monster with eyes in the back of its head and arms coming out of its ears was going to creep into my room in the middle of the night and steal one of my arms or legs and hide it in the watermelon patch."

Noah says there was no protection from the Watermelon Baby. "I just had to lie there every night and hope he didn't choose me."

Another friend had a six-fingered witch in her closet. As long as the light was on in the closet, the witch couldn't appear.

Michael had a wild monster-dog that hid under his bed. The only thing that could tame the dog was Michael's mother's voice. So, until he fell asleep, he called his mother every half hour.

In collecting personal monster stories, I heard tales about TV heroes, movie witches, cartoon characters, and comic strip ghouls who haunted night bedrooms.

And many people talked about being scared of eerie shadows on moonlit nights; of howling winds and tapping rain; of pictures on their walls and things hanging in the room.

And to protect themselves from these monsters, people pulled sheets up to their chins or hid under their blankets. And lots of my friends had night-lights, closet lights, and perpetually locked windows.

And finally there's Lewis. His worst night creature only lasted a few weeks, but it was memorable.

When Lewis was eight years old, he spent one entire day watching a Dracula movie, over and over again. By bedtime he was paralyzed with fear. He wouldn't let his mother leave the room. And he couldn't possibly close his eyes for fear that Dracula would appear.

Finally, in desperation, his mother cut out four crosses from construction paper and taped one to each side of the bed. Then, as added insurance, she hung a clove of garlic over his head.

"I slept like that for weeks," says Lewis with a laugh.

The more people Nancy and I talked to, the more intrigued we became. Most everyone had something to say on the subject. So we decided to let the reader write the final chapter.

Write as much as you want . . . in as much detail as you can. Describe your monsters. Write about how you feel when you lie in bed at night, what you're afraid will happen, what you do to protect yourself. If you know where you got the idea of your night monster (TV, an older brother, a fairy tale, etc.), write that, too.

If, by some chance, you don't have any night monsters of your own, write about someone else's.

And if you like, make a copy of your story and send it to us, along with your name and address, in care of the publisher of our book. We'd love to read it.

Good luck!

My Personal Night Monster

by _____

Bibliography

Vampires

Aylesworth, Thomas G. *The Story of Vampires*. New York: Lippincott, 1977.

Dresser, Norline. *American Vampires: Fans, Victims, Practitioners*. New York & London: W.W. Norton & Company, 1989.

Encyclopedia of Occultism and Parapsychology. 2nd Edition. Detroit: Gale Research Company, 1984.

McHargue, Georgess. *Meet the Vampire*. Philadelphia: Lippincott, 1979.

Robbin, Rossell Hope. *Encyclopedia of Witchcraft and Demonology*. New York: Bonanza Books, 1959.

Summers, Montague. *The Vampire: His Kith and Kin*. New Hyde Park, New York: University Books, 1960.

Underwood, Peter. *The Vampire's Bedside Companion*. London: Frewin, 1975.

Werewolves

Aylesworth, Thomas G. *The Story of Werewolves*. New York: McGraw-Hill, 1978.

Cooper, Basil. *The Werewolf: In Legend, Fact and Art*. New York: St. Martin's Press, 1977.

McHargue, Georgess. *Meet the Werewolf*. Philadelphia: Lippincott, 1976.

Otten, Charlotte F. *A Lycanthropy Reader: Werewolves in Western Culture*. Syracuse: Syracuse University Press, 1986.

Summers, Montague. *The Werewolf*. Secaucus, New Jersey: The Citadel Press, 1966.

Yolen, Jane, and Martin H. Greenberg. *Werewolves*. New York: Harper & Row, 1988.